Into the FOREST

Story by Tania Cox

Illustrations by Isabelle Duffy

Into the Forest

Text: Tania Cox
Publishers: Tania Mazzeo and Eliza Webb
Series consultant: Amanda Sutera
Hands on Heads Consulting
Editor: Kate Daniel
Project editor: Annabel Smith
Designer: Jess Kelly
Project designer: Danielle Maccarone
Illustrations: Isabelle Duffy
Production controller: Renee Tome

NovaStar

ISBN 978 0 17 033484 6

Cengage Learning Australia
Level 5, 80 Dorcas Street
Southbank VIC 3006 Australia
Phone: 1300 790 853
Email: aust.nelsonprimary@cengage.com

For learning solutions, visit **cengage.com.au**

Printed in China by 1010 Printing International Ltd
1 2 3 4 5 6 7 29 28 27 26 25

Nelson acknowledges the Traditional Owners and Custodians of the lands of all First Nations Peoples. We pay respect to Elders past and present, and extend that respect to all First Nations Peoples today.

Contents

Author's Note

I've always loved the lush, shadowy forests of North Queensland and the vocal wildlife that lives there. I especially love the mysterious feeling of the unknown that sweeps over you as you walk deeper into the forest. I do lots of thinking while walking.

On one of those forest walks, I started to think about how long some of the trees had been here. A very long time! Then I thought about the Traditional Owners of the land, who have also been here a very long time, telling their Dreaming stories about the forests and the creatures that might live there. One particular great tall hairy creature sprang to mind. The yowie! I hope you enjoy the journey into the forest with Charlie, Lucy and Bubbles.

I dedicate this book to the Juru people, past, present and the future, for allowing the use of their yowie folklore in this story, and to North Queensland's forests, for being an inspiration.

Chapter 1

Eavesdropping

Sometimes, strange things happen that not even parents can explain.

Charlie discovered this fact late one night in his new home. He couldn't sleep. He tossed and turned in bed. Finally, he got up and tiptoed out of his bedroom. He closed the door on Bubbles the dog, snoring loudly at the foot of his bed. Charlie's family had inherited the demanding, yappy dog and an in-the-middle-of-nowhere cattle property from Great-Uncle Percy. Worst of all, now that they'd moved onto the property, in a few days Charlie would have to start at a new school! No wonder he couldn't sleep.

I'll treat my new-school-can't-sleep worries to a cup of hot chocolate, he thought, moving towards the stairs.

His parents' voices drifted up from the kitchen. Charlie heard his name mentioned. He stopped and immediately sat down on the top step. He knew eavesdropping was wrong. *But what are they saying about me?* he wondered, frowning.

The discussion couldn't be about him having the messiest room on the planet, as his parents always used to say. Charlie had no choice now but to be tidy, because Bubbles shredded anything that was left on the floor.

Charlie had even taped drawings on the wall at dog's eye level to show Bubbles what she was supposed to chew and not chew. But she'd shredded the drawings too. Mum explained the dog's naughtiness was probably because Bubbles missed Great-Uncle Percy. Mum had grown up with Great-Uncle Percy, and she missed him the most out of everyone – but she didn't go around chewing everything to bits!

Snatches of his parents' conversation wafted up towards Charlie.

"Just got off ... phone," said Dad. "Can't explain ... calves disappearing." "... lives in the forest."

Then Charlie heard Mum say, "... keep Charlie out ... make trap."

Chairs rumbled as they were moved on the wooden floor. Bolts slid and clunked across doors, and lights were switched off.

"Try to get some sleep," Dad finally said.

Their bedroom door clicked shut below.

What was that about? thought Charlie, heading quietly down the stairs. He had so much to tell his hot chocolate. And it wasn't just about new-school worries.

Chapter 2

Footprints

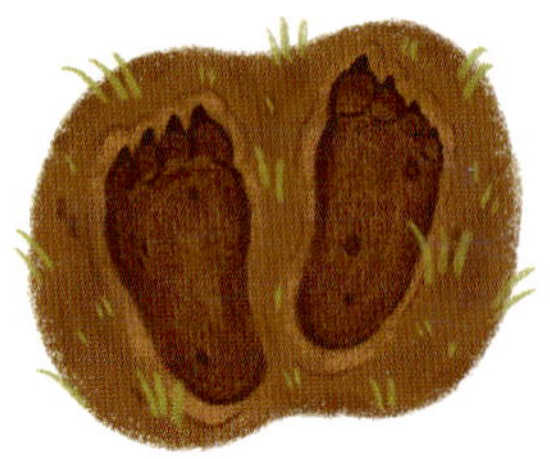

The next morning, Charlie took Bubbles for a walk. Bubbles pulled on the lead and pounced at bugs.

Charlie hadn't walked far when he saw his neighbour Lucy riding her horse towards him. Lucy went to the same school Charlie would be attending.

Charlie bent down to unclip Bubbles's lead, to let her run free.

"Keep her on her lead," Lucy called out, getting down from her horse.

"Why?" asked Charlie. Bubbles seemed to love her freedom.

"Follow me. I'll show you," said Lucy, tying the horse to a fence post.

Charlie shrugged and checked Bubbles's lead was still secured. He wiggled through the fence with the dog. Both properties had fenced-off blocks which backed onto a lush, green forest. Charlie followed Lucy through the open, grassy paddock until she stopped.

Lucy pointed to some flat brown patches in the grass.

Charlie stared. They were footprints, around three times the size of Dad's. "Who or what made them?" Charlie gasped.

“These are yowie footprints,” said Lucy. “My nan’s ancestors have been here since the Dreaming. Nan grew up hearing about great tall hairy creatures called yowies living in the forest and roaming at night.” Lucy nodded towards the forest. “Some kids in my class call that Yowie Forest.”

Charlie shuddered. Enormous footprints meant enormous yowies! “Lucy, do you really think yowies exist?” he asked. But he had a feeling that he already knew the answer as he stared down at the clear footprints.

“I believe the stories of my ancestors,” Lucy said. “Last night, two of our calves went missing. My dad found these footprints and phoned your parents to warn them about a yowie possibly taking the calves.”

Charlie nodded, remembering the bits of his parents’ conversation that he’d heard last night.

“So, hang on tight to Bubbles’s lead,” said Lucy, “and don’t let her go into …” But before Lucy could finish, a butterfly fluttered past.

Bubbles bolted, yanking her lead out of Charlie’s hand. She chased the butterfly across the paddock, under the next fence and straight into Yowie Forest.

Chapter 3

Yowie Forest

"Bubbles! Come back!" cried Charlie. His brain screamed at him to chase after her, but his legs wouldn't cooperate. They preferred to shake rather than run into Yowie Forest.

"Quick! Let's get Bubbles out of there!" shouted Lucy, racing off after the dog.

Charlie slapped his legs into action, and he followed Lucy along a narrow dirt track into the shadowy Yowie Forest. "Bubbles!" he panted.

Charlie caught up to Lucy, who'd stopped running and was waiting for him.

"Let's walk slowly from here," said Lucy. "We don't want to miss anything."

"Like massive footprints? I doubt if we could miss them!" Charlie said.

"No," Lucy said. "Like Bubbles's paw prints in the track. Or the sound of her whimpering."

"Whimpering? Poor Bubbles." Charlie wanted to find Bubbles safe and then get out of Yowie Forest – fast! He looked around. Sunlight trickled through the treetops to the ground. Crickets and birds chirped out as if they were in a singing competition. It would be hard to hear Bubbles's whimpering if she was hurt.

“Do yowies make a particular sound?” asked Charlie, listening hard for any unusual noise.

“Nan says they grunt,” Lucy said. Suddenly, she stopped walking. “Down there!”

Charlie quickly got down so low to the ground, he almost hugged it.

“I meant *look* down there,” said Lucy, pointing to the track. “Not get down.”

“I was just getting ready to have a super close look,” replied Charlie, standing up shakily.

Lucy crouched near some small paw prints. "These could belong to Bubbles," she said. "Nan and I go walking through Country a lot, and we look for prints all the time. Nan always knows what's made them."

Just then, familiar yapping filled the air.

"Bubbles!" shouted Charlie. "That's her happy yap when she plays!" He raced off in the direction of the sound.

Charlie and Lucy followed the sound deeper into the forest. They entered a clearing and found Bubbles at the base of a huge bunya tree. Bubbles had her head tilted back, barking up at the tree. Her tail wagged so quickly, it was blurry.

"Bubbles!" Charlie said with relief. "I never thought I'd be so happy to see you! Come on, girl. Let's go home."

But Bubbles kept yapping and wagging her tail at the tree. She wouldn't budge.

"What's Bubbles barking at?" asked Lucy, looking around.

Charlie shrugged. "Don't know. Maybe another butterfly." He bit his lip, glancing around at the shadowy forest.

At that moment, a bunya cone fell to the forest floor with a loud *whump*. Bubbles rushed to it and sniffed it in a frenzy.

Charlie crouched close to Bubbles and picked up the lead. “Forget about that bunya cone, Bubbles. How about a TREAT?”

Bubbles took off so fast at the sound of her favourite word, Charlie’s feet left the ground!

Lucy laughed and followed them out of the forest.

Charlie never knew he could run so fast. He was breathing hard when they all got back to where Lucy’s horse was tied. Charlie quickly waved goodbye to Lucy as Bubbles dragged him towards the house.

Back at home, Charlie took Bubbles off the lead and walked straight into the kitchen to get her a treat. A note was stuck to the fridge.

Charlie,

Dad's in town. I'm in the far paddock. We'll both be back around lunchtime. DO NOT GO INTO THE FOREST! *Talk after lunch.*

Mum x

"A bit late for that warning," huffed Charlie, reaching into the cupboard for the bag of Yummy-O's. "Treat time!" he said to the dog.

But Bubbles ran upstairs. Charlie frowned. Normally Bubbles stuck to him like glue until he gave her a promised treat.

Happy yapping came from his bedroom.

Charlie walked up the stairs and into his room. "Bubbles!" he called. "Here's your …" Then he saw in the corner of his bedroom what Bubbles was yapping at.

He dropped the treat to the floor. And froze.

Chapter 4

An Open Window

Charlie trembled from the tips of his hair to the tips of his toenails. He stared without blinking at the small, short, hairy and human-like creature standing in the corner of his room.

Charlie remembered what Lucy's nan had told Lucy about yowies. Great. Tall. Hairy. But what stood in front of Charlie was small, short and hairy! Could it be a yowie?

Charlie looked down at the creature's feet. They were big, although not big enough to create those footprints in the paddock. *But a larger version of this waist-high hairy thing could definitely make those footprints*, he thought.

"Goo-goo. Coo-coo," gurgled the creature, as Bubbles rubbed against its furry body.

It sort of sounds like a baby, thought Charlie. *Is it a baby yowie?*

As Charlie watched, the baby yowie seemed to finally notice him. It lifted its eyes from his feet up to his face. It jolted and its eyes widened.

A mild breeze drifted in through the open window and swept over Charlie. *Baby Yowie must've climbed up the tree and through the window this morning*, he thought.

Then something else flashed across Charlie's mind, making his stomach feel like someone had dropped a bowling ball right to the bottom of it. If this was a baby yowie, then where was its mother? Or its father?

The thought of Mama or Papa Yowie tracking down their baby to Charlie's house, and then squeezing through his window, was terrifying. It made Charlie want to return Baby Yowie to its home faster than Bubbles vanishing at her least favourite word: "vet".

But he would need help to do it.

Baby Yowie and Bubbles seemed to be playing some sort of tug-of-war game with a rope toy.

Charlie walked at snail's pace over to the window and gently closed it. Then he backed slowly out of his room and carefully shut the door.

"Now to get some expert yowie advice!" he decided. And Charlie knew exactly who to run to.

Chapter 5

Jelly Legs

Lucy was coming out of the stables on her family's property when Charlie found her.

"Lucy!" he called, gulping for air.

"Charlie," she said. "Calm down. You look like you've seen a ..."

"Yowie!" cried Charlie. "I've seen a yowie! Quick! Follow me!"

When they got back to Charlie's room, Baby Yowie was sitting on the floor gurgling as Bubbles tried to nibble at its feet.

Lucy gasped when she walked in. Then she slowly crouched. "What brings you here, cute little hairy one?" she said softly.

Charlie made a face. He didn't know why Baby Yowie was here. He didn't know if he thought it was cute, either.

Bubbles nuzzled Baby Yowie under its arm, then yapped happily.

"That's it!" blurted Charlie. "I know why Baby Yowie is here! It's Bubbles! When we found Bubbles in the forest, she was making happy yaps at something up the bunya tree. It mustn't have been at a butterfly. It must've been at Baby Yowie. Maybe they'd been playing together before we arrived."

Lucy smiled. "Ahh, Baby Yowie, you came here looking for your playmate."

A nervous thought flickered across Charlie's mind. "Lucy, you know what this means, don't you?"

Lucy stood up carefully. "Yowie Forest," she said, "here we come again!"

"Back to the bunya tree Baby Yowie came from," said Charlie.

Charlie's legs turned to jelly at the idea of going back to Yowie Forest, but he started for the door. He shuddered at the thought of Mama or Papa Yowie climbing through his window to get their baby.

Charlie glanced at a photo on his chest of drawers of Mum cuddling him as a toddler. He hoped she'd understand why he had to go back into the forest after she'd told him not to.

Bubbles was chewing on a squeaky toy ball, watching Baby Yowie out of one eye. The yowie reached playfully for the toy, but Bubbles wiggled out of reach.

Just then, Charlie shook the lead and Bubbles raced over. She dropped the ball at his feet, and Charlie picked it up. "Thanks, Bubbles. This might be useful," he said. He turned towards Baby Yowie and squeaked the ball. "Let's take you home, little hairy one."

They walked through the paddocks back to the forest. Baby Yowie trotted alongside Bubbles, following Charlie and Lucy.

When they entered the forest, Charlie looked around. All the trees looked the same. “Lucy, I can’t remember exactly where we found Bubbles.”

Lucy pointed down at the dirt track. “We’ll follow our morning footprints through the forest,” she said. “Look – our shoe prints.”

Charlie stared down at the path and gulped. “I hope there are no new, big footprints!”

“I hope we don’t hear any loud whacks on a tree,” said Lucy. “Nan says that’s usually a sign that a yowie is close by. Or a strong smell like a wet dog. That’s a sign too.”

Charlie shuddered for the millionth time that day.

Soon their morning footprints led them to the bunya tree where they had found Bubbles.

"Off you go, Baby Yowie, you're home now," Charlie said. He took the toy ball from his pocket, squeaked it twice, then rolled it along the ground into the bushes.

Baby Yowie wobbled after it.

"Quick, Lucy, let's head back," whispered Charlie, turning around and tugging at Bubbles's lead.

Then, behind them, a loud grunting noise boomed through the trees.

Charlie's legs went to jelly once more.

Chapter 6

Hero, Not Villain

A humungous version of Baby Yowie came thundering towards him, looking incredibly hairy and, worst of all, incredibly angry! There was no doubt in Charlie's mind, it was a ...

"Yowie!" he screamed. "Run!" Charlie didn't know if he was screaming to Lucy or to his legs! His jelly legs had frosted over now, freezing him to the spot. Bubbles half growled, half whimpered, but mostly hid behind Charlie. Charlie was holding onto Bubbles's lead so tightly, his knuckles turned white.

"Charlie!" yelled Lucy. "Come on!"

"Too scared to move!" Charlie groaned, as the yowie's footsteps thumped louder and closer.

Then from behind a nearby rock came long, deep growls.

“What was that?” gasped Charlie, looking over at the rock.

Baby Yowie scrambled out of the bushes and clambered up the bunya tree.

Lucy ran back to Charlie, grabbing his arm and yanking him into a run. “Come on!” she yelled again.

Charlie stumbled over a protruding tree root and dropped Bubbles’s lead, but Lucy quickly scooped it up.

Three skinny wild dogs, baring sharp, jagged teeth, leapt out over the rock towards Bubbles.

The huge yowie pounded past Charlie and lunged straight at the snarling dogs. A second later, the dogs bolted away, yelping.

Charlie stood up, his heart pounding as if it would beat right out of his chest. All he wanted to do was go home. But the huge yowie blocked the path home. A strong smell like wet dog filled Charlie's nostrils. He trembled.

Charlie looked at Lucy. She was motionless, just staring at the enormous yowie, with her mouth gaping. It seemed it was Lucy's turn now to be frozen with fear. Charlie looked down at Bubbles - she seemed frozen with fear as well!

Baby Yowie climbed down from the tree. It gurgled "mmm" sounds as it headed quickly past Charlie, with hairy arms outstretched to the huge yowie.

Must be its mama, thought Charlie. He smiled weakly. Maybe it was the fact that Mama Yowie had saved Bubbles or that she was hugging Baby Yowie, but she didn't seem so scary now. *Still scary*, thought Charlie. *Just not THAT scary.*

"Come on, Lucy," he whispered. "Let's go."

Lucy nodded, still staring at the yowies.

Charlie moved slowly towards Mama Yowie and her baby. He tried hard not to rustle any leaf litter.

Please let us pass, Charlie thought, taking another step forward.

Just as he did, he could feel eyes watching him. He looked up.

Mama Yowie was regarding Charlie curiously.

Charlie stopped. Mama Yowie still blocked his path. Baby Yowie was snuggled against her neck sucking its thumb.

"C … c … can you please move?" said Charlie. "Home. I need to go home." He pointed towards the way out of the forest. He hoped Mama Yowie would move just a little, so they could get past.

Mama Yowie grunted. She pointed in the same direction and grunted again.

“Charlie,” whispered Lucy, “she doesn’t understand English, just like we don’t understand Yowie-ish.”

“Good point,” said Charlie. Suddenly, he had an idea. Maybe drawing a picture would work better with Mama Yowie than it had with Bubbles. He picked up a stick and drew a square with a triangle on top in the dirt. “Home. I need to go home,” he said again.

Mama Yowie grunted. She crouched down. She picked up a stick and drew in the dirt too.

Her drawing looked like two triangles with little triangles inside. Near the triangles, she drew some wonky semicircles.

“What on earth is that? A beak with teeth?” said Charlie, guessing wildly. But he had no idea what the semicircles were supposed to be.

Just then, loud animal bleating could be heard coming from the direction of home.

Mama Yowie turned sideways to where the noise came from, leaving just enough room for Charlie, Lucy and Bubbles to pass.

"Nice meeting you, Mama and Baby Yowie," Charlie said. "See you!" He was nearly going to add "later" on the end, but honestly, even though he wasn't *that* scared of them now, he would prefer never to see them again!

By the time Charlie, Lucy and Bubbles arrived back at the paddock near Great-Uncle Percy's house, high-pitched mooing pierced the air. In the far corner, some cattle were huddled together. Charlie's stomach churned as he saw why. "Look, Lucy!" he cried.

The three wild dogs were circling the cows.

"Get away!" shouted Charlie.

One of the dogs crept close to a calf. It nipped at the calf's leg. But a bigger cow kicked it away. The dog approached another calf.

"STOP!" yelled Lucy.

Just then, Charlie heard a loud grunting sound. A huge shape burst out of the forest! Mama Yowie! She leapt over the fence and thundered her way through the paddock. She lunged at the dogs, chasing them away.

Charlie and Lucy looked at each other.

"Mama Yowie has been *saving* the calves. Not taking them!" gasped Charlie. "That's why her footprints were in your paddock, Lucy!" He remembered the drawings. Were the triangles a dog's snout with sharp teeth? Were the wonky semicircles cow horns?

"Goo-goo! Coo-coo!" Baby Yowie wobbled out of the forest and into view.

Mama Yowie changed direction and raced towards Baby Yowie. As she passed under a gum tree, a thick net on the ground scooped up Mama Yowie and left her dangling from a branch.

Chapter 7

Trapped

Mama Yowie howled and yowled, thrashing in the net. Baby Yowie arrived moments later. Mama Yowie stopped thrashing when she saw her baby staring up at her.

When Charlie, Lucy and Bubbles got to the trap, Mama Yowie was bunched up and looking at them with very frightened eyes.

"Don't worry," Charlie said softly. "We won't let anything happen to you."

"Or to Baby Yowie," said Lucy, stepping closer to the net.

Bubbles nuzzled Baby Yowie.

Charlie and Lucy pulled hard at the trap that enclosed Mama Yowie. Charlie shook his head. "It's no use, Lucy. We need help to free Mama Yowie."

At that moment, wheels spun in the dirt. Doors slammed. Charlie turned around to see Mum and Dad running towards him through the paddock.

“Kids! Get inside!” shouted Mum.

“I’m calling the police!” yelled Dad.

“No!” said Charlie. “You can’t!”

Mum and Dad skidded to a stop. “It’s enormous! And hairy!” gulped Dad. “And, ugh – smelly.”

“Is that a baby one too?” gasped Mum.

“Yes, Mama Yowie is enormous, hairy and smells like Bubbles after she’s swum in the swamp,” Charlie blurted. “And yes, there’s a baby yowie too! But please don’t call anyone until we explain.”

Charlie quickly told his parents about how Mama Yowie was saving the calves from the wild dogs.

"She saved Bubbles too!" said Lucy.

Mum and Dad shook their heads. They looked at each other and then turned away to have a hushed discussion. It seemed to end with them both nodding. Dad reached for his phone.

"Help us save Mama Yowie, now," begged Charlie.

"Please let the yowies go back into the forest peacefully," pleaded Lucy. "Nan says drawing attention to them would bring hunters into the forest."

Dad dialled the number of the police.

"No!" cried Charlie.

Chapter 8

Hot Chocolate

"I'd like to report wild dogs in the area," Dad said.

Charlie and Lucy listened with bated breath as Dad made his report to the police. Finally, he hung up the phone. He hadn't mentioned the yowies at all.

"Yes!" cheered Charlie, turning to Mama Yowie. "Time for you and Baby Yowie to go home!"

After carefully lowering and unknotting the net, they finally freed Mama Yowie from the trap. Baby Yowie ran straight into its mama's arms for a big yowie hug. Then Mama Yowie swung Baby Yowie up onto her shoulders. She looked at Charlie and pointed to the forest.

"Over there?" asked Charlie, pointing in the same direction. "Is that your home?"

With Baby Yowie still on her shoulders, Mama Yowie knelt and scratched another picture in the dirt. It sort of looked like an upside-down letter "V".

Charlie looked again to where she'd been pointing before. He looked beyond the forest and into the distance. "Oh," said Charlie, slowly. "You're heading to the mountains. So that's what you drew."

Mama Yowie grunted, then started walking towards the forest. Baby Yowie gave Bubbles one last look before turning away.

Bubbles whimpered.

Charlie patted her gently. "Poor Bubbles, you've lost your friend," he said.

Together with Mum, Dad, Lucy and Bubbles, Charlie watched Mama Yowie and Baby Yowie disappear into Yowie Forest.

"I think we all need to go home for a nice, strong hot chocolate with triple marshmallows," said Mum. "We'll keep watch from the verandah for the wild dogs."

"Those dogs won't be back in a hurry," said Lucy. "Mama Yowie gave them a good fright."

Dad looked back at the forest and shuddered. "I admit it. They weren't the only ones she gave a good fright."

Charlie smiled, walking back to the house with them. He hoped the yowies would be able to live peacefully in the forest without people being terrified of them. *Imagine if Baby Yowie walked into my new school!* he thought.

Oh, school. Charlie sighed. He'd forgotten about starting at a new school. At least Lucy would be there.

As he walked into the kitchen, Charlie saw Bubbles wrestling with one of his socks. "I won't miss you while I'm at school, Bubbles," said Charlie with a smile, giving her a treat anyway and a pat. "Well, maybe just a little."

"But seriously," Charlie told his hot chocolate, "after coming face to face with yowies and wild dogs today, maybe starting at a new school won't be so scary after all." He picked up the cup and headed out to the verandah where Mum, Dad and Lucy sat. *Still scary*, he thought. *Just not* THAT *scary*.